101 Ghost Stories

MOONSTONE

Published in Moonstone
by Rupa Publications India Pvt. Ltd 2025
7/16, Ansari Road, Daryaganj
New Delhi 110002

Sales centres:
Bengaluru Chennai
Hyderabad Jaipur Kathmandu
Kolkata Mumbai Prayagraj

P-ISBN: 978-93-7003-140-1
E-ISBN: 978-93-7003-154-8

First impression 2025

10 9 8 7 6 5 4 3 2 1

CONTENTS

CONTENTS

1. The Photograph with Blinking Eyes (Italy)

In Nonna's hallway hung a photo of a girl in black and white. "That's Lucia," Nonna whispered. "She died young, but she watches over us." When Sofia walked by, she could swear Lucia's eyes followed her. One day, she blinked. Just once. Sofia dropped her juice. "She's friendly," Nonna said. "Wave next

time." Sofia did. The photo girl smiled faintly. Another day, she winked. During a thunderstorm, the lights went out—except around Lucia's frame. Her smile widened. After that, Sofia always greeted her. And Lucia always watched back, eyes warm, like an old friend keeping quiet, eternal company.

2. The Lantern of Kyoto (Japan)

In a quiet Kyoto alley, Hiro saw a red lantern glowing without a flame. Curious, he followed its path night after night. One evening, the lantern floated into a garden where an old woman smiled. "You found me," she whispered. "I waited many years." She served him tea and stories until dawn. But when Hiro returned the next night, only a cold, empty teacup remained. The lantern never glowed again. Still, every spring, a red light flickers in the garden. Locals say it's the spirit waiting for another friend brave enough to follow the light.

3. The Whistling Woods (Scotland)

Children in the Highlands are told never to whistle in the woods. "It wakes them," old folk warn. But Eilidh didn't believe it. One autumn afternoon, she skipped into the forest and whistled a happy tune. Trees rustled. The wind stopped. Then the woods began to whistle back—soft, high-pitched, eerie. The sounds followed her, circling like a game. She ran, heart pounding. At the forest's edge, she cried, "I'm sorry!" The whistling faded. Now, whenever wind rushes through those trees, locals wonder—is it wind, or something still waiting for a song?

4. Midnight Mangoes (India)

Hee hee
heee hee'

Ravi loved mangoes more than anything. One summer night, he crept into his neighbour's orchard under the full moon. Just as he reached for a ripe mango, the tree whispered, "Hungry?" Startled, he stumbled back. The fruit lifted into the air, glowing gold. Mangoes danced in circles, giggling with tiny ghostly voices. Ravi ran, but every night after, a mango appeared on his pillow—ripe, sweet, and warm. Years later, he tells kids to never steal. "But if a mango floats to you," he says, "say thank you. It means the orchard spirits like you."

5. The Canal Girl (Netherlands)

On frozen winter nights, a glowing girl skates the canals of Amsterdam. Clara saw her once while sipping cocoa near the window. The girl glided silently, dressed in old-fashioned clothes, never blinking. Curious, Clara stepped outside and waved. The girl waved back—then vanished into thin air. The next morning, Clara found an old ice skate at her door with her name carved into it, even though she'd never skated before. Locals say if the Canal Girl waves at you, she leaves behind a gift... or a mystery. Clara still keeps the skate, waiting for her to return.

6. Grandma's Rocking Chair (USA)

After Grandma passed, Milly stayed in her old room for the summer. Every night, the rocking chair moved on its own, creaking slowly. Milly tried to ignore it—until she smelled lavender, Grandma's favourite scent. One night, the chair rocked faster, and Milly heard soft humming. "Grandma?" she whispered. The chair stopped. From then on, she said "Goodnight, Grandma" before bed, and the chair gently rocked once in reply. When summer ended, the chair never moved again. But Milly always believed her grandma stayed with her, one final summer of love and lullabies.

"Grandma?"

7. The Lost Violinist (Italy)

In Venice, Leo wandered off from his school trip, following beautiful violin music echoing through the alleyways. He found a pale boy dressed in old clothes, playing beneath a flickering lantern. "I used to play for crowds," the ghost said. "But they forgot me." Leo clapped and said, "You're amazing." The boy smiled, bowed, and slowly faded into mist. When Leo returned to the group, no one believed his story— until he opened his backpack to find a miniature violin inside, with a note: *Grazie.* Every year, Leo visits that alley, hoping to hear the music again.

Tourists in Cairo love the pyramids, but few notice the glowing green-eyed cat that prowls nearby at night. Samira did. The cat sat beside her, purring like thunder. She reached out to pet it—but her hand passed through. It blinked slowly and walked through a solid wall. The next morning, Samira asked the guide, who smiled and whispered, "A pharaoh's cat. Still guarding treasures." Since then, Samira leaves a bit of fish near the spot each visit. It always disappears. Some say the cat chooses a child every century to share its secrets.

9. The Pirate of Port Royal (Jamaica)

Caleb loved collecting shells near the shore. One moonlit night, he heard, "Polly?" over the crashing waves. A ghostly pirate limped across the sand, searching for his parrot. Caleb froze as the pirate turned. "Seen her?" he asked, holding a broken perch. Caleb shook his head. The pirate sighed and faded. Feeling sorry, Caleb returned the next night with a toy parrot. He left it on the rocks. It vanished by morning. The ghost was never seen again—but sometimes, people hear a happy squawk and a jolly "Aye!" echoing across the bay.

10. The Umbrella Lady (England)

On a rainy London afternoon, Lucy found a bright red umbrella resting against a lamppost. A woman nearby smiled and said, "Keep it dry." Lucy took it home. But one day, she left it open in the rain. That night, her shoes vanished. Then her socks. Each night, something else disappeared—her schoolbag, her teddy. Panicked, Lucy dried the umbrella carefully and whispered, "I'm sorry." Everything returned. Now, she always takes care of it. And every rainy day, a different child finds the Umbrella Lady waiting, offering them the same warning: "Keep it dry."

11. The Whispering Train (South Africa)

In the dry Karoo desert, there's an old railway with no trains. But every month, under a full moon, children say they hear a whistle blow and the sound of wheels on invisible tracks. Sipho, curious and brave, stayed up one night and waved at the sound. A soft breeze whooshed past, and a golden ticket fluttered into his hands. It read: *Karoo Ghost Express – One Ride Only.* He blinked, and the ticket vanished. No one believes him, but sometimes, when the moon is just right, he swears he hears, "All aboard!"

12. The Mirror Market (Morocco)

In Marrakech, Layla found a strange mirror at a market stall. Her reflection smiled when she didn't. "That's not me," she whispered. At home, the mirror showed her doing things she'd never done—climbing trees, dancing in the rain. One night, her reflection waved and mouthed, "Come play." Layla blinked—and was gone. The mirror was empty. Her parents found her laughing outside, soaked with rain. But they never bought mirrors again. Some say the mirror shows your brave side. Others say it steals you... if you forget who you are.

13. The Balloon from Berlin (Germany)

Felix let go of his red balloon in the park. It drifted high, then disappeared into a cloudy sky. That night, the balloon tapped his bedroom window—tied to a tiny envelope. Inside was a drawing he didn't make. Every night, the balloon returned, each time with a new picture. One showed Felix laughing with a ghostly boy wearing the same pyjamas. "He had no one to play with," whispered Felix. After a week, the balloon stopped coming. But Felix still keeps the drawings under his bed—and sometimes dreams of flying.

14. The Singing Steps (Ireland)

At her granddad's old cottage, Niamh heard singing on the stairs. "Go to sleep," her mum said. But the voice was soft, warm, and very old. Niamh tiptoed out and saw faint footprints glowing blue. She followed them down the steps to an empty chair, gently rocking. The singing stopped. On the cushion was a music box she'd never seen. It played the same tune. Granddad said the house once belonged to a kind woman who sang children to sleep. Niamh smiled, wound the box, and listened. The stairs haven't sung since.

15. The Bus to Nowhere (Canada)

In snowy Quebec, Jonah missed his school bus and found another waiting at the stop. No driver. No lights. But the door opened. He stepped in. Other children sat quietly, eyes closed. As the bus moved, fog rolled outside. "Where are we going?" Jonah whispered. "Back," said a girl. "Back where?" She smiled. "Before." Panicking, Jonah pressed the stop button. The bus screeched and disappeared. He woke up at the stop, safe. Since then, he never misses the bus. Because once, he nearly rode with children who were never meant to return.

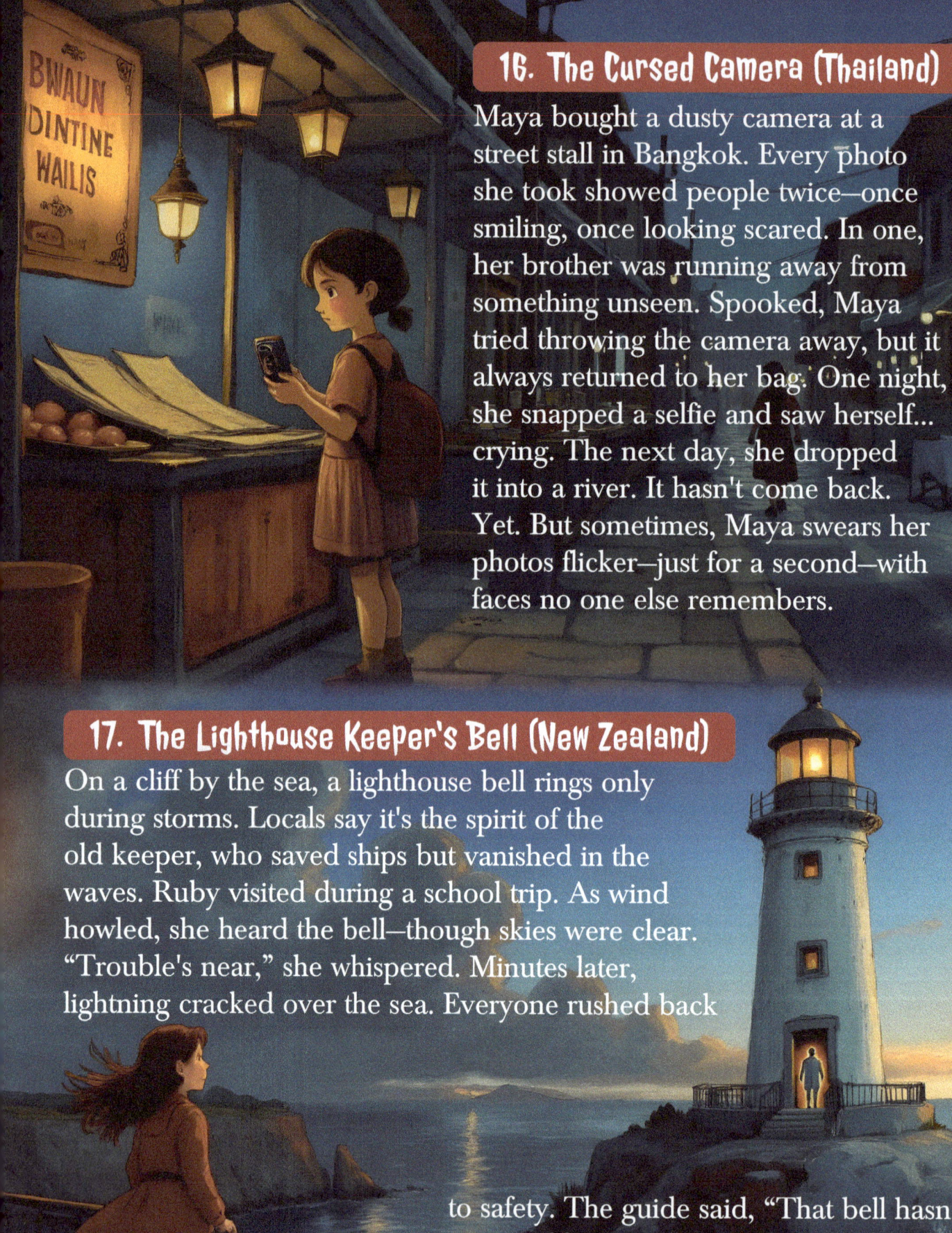

16. The Cursed Camera (Thailand)

Maya bought a dusty camera at a street stall in Bangkok. Every photo she took showed people twice—once smiling, once looking scared. In one, her brother was running away from something unseen. Spooked, Maya tried throwing the camera away, but it always returned to her bag. One night, she snapped a selfie and saw herself... crying. The next day, she dropped it into a river. It hasn't come back. Yet. But sometimes, Maya swears her photos flicker—just for a second—with faces no one else remembers.

17. The Lighthouse Keeper's Bell (New Zealand)

On a cliff by the sea, a lighthouse bell rings only during storms. Locals say it's the spirit of the old keeper, who saved ships but vanished in the waves. Ruby visited during a school trip. As wind howled, she heard the bell—though skies were clear. "Trouble's near," she whispered. Minutes later, lightning cracked over the sea. Everyone rushed back to safety. The guide said, "That bell hasn't rung in fifty years." Ruby turned toward the lighthouse. A figure stood there, saluting her. Then, he vanished into the wind.

18. The Floating Shoes (Brazil)

In a Rio de Janeiro shop, Leo tried on shiny dancing shoes. They felt light—too light. That night, they danced by themselves in his room, spinning and tapping. When Leo wore them again, they danced *with* him. He couldn't stop! Music played from nowhere, his feet moved without control. Laughing and terrified, he yanked them off. They hovered, then dropped to the floor. The next morning, the shoes were gone. But the rhythm stayed in his head, and sometimes... his toes tap to music only he can hear.

19. The Invisible Zoo (Kenya)

Amani's school visited Nairobi's museum, but she wandered off. She found a hidden gate marked: *Ghost Safari*. Inside, there were no animals—but rustling, pawprints, roars. She felt a warm snout nuzzle her hand. A voice said, "Thank you for remembering us." When she returned, her shoes were muddy, and she held a feather that shimmered like silver. No one else saw the gate. But Amani drew pictures of creatures no one recognised.

Her teacher said, "They don't exist." Amani smiled. "They do. You just have to believe."

20. The Library Clock (Russia)

In Saint Petersburg's old library, a massive clock ticks backward. When Nadia touched it, everything froze—except her. A whisper echoed: "You have five minutes." She wandered past still readers, frozen birds mid-flight, and paused by a dusty book titled *Your Story*. She opened it—and saw pages of her future. Scared, she closed it and ran back. The clock ticked once—and the world moved again. She never spoke of it, but each birthday, she writes a page of her own story. Just in case the clock ever ticks backwards again.

21. The Paintbrush of Dreams (France)

At an antique shop in Paris, Amélie found an old paintbrush. That night, she painted a door on her wall—and it opened. She stepped through into a world made of colours, where clouds were cotton candy and ghosts danced like shadows. One ghost, kind and quiet, gave her a painting of herself smiling. "For when you forget," he said. She woke up with the painting in her hands. The brush never worked again. But Amélie became an artist, painting dreams no one else could imagine—except maybe that ghost.

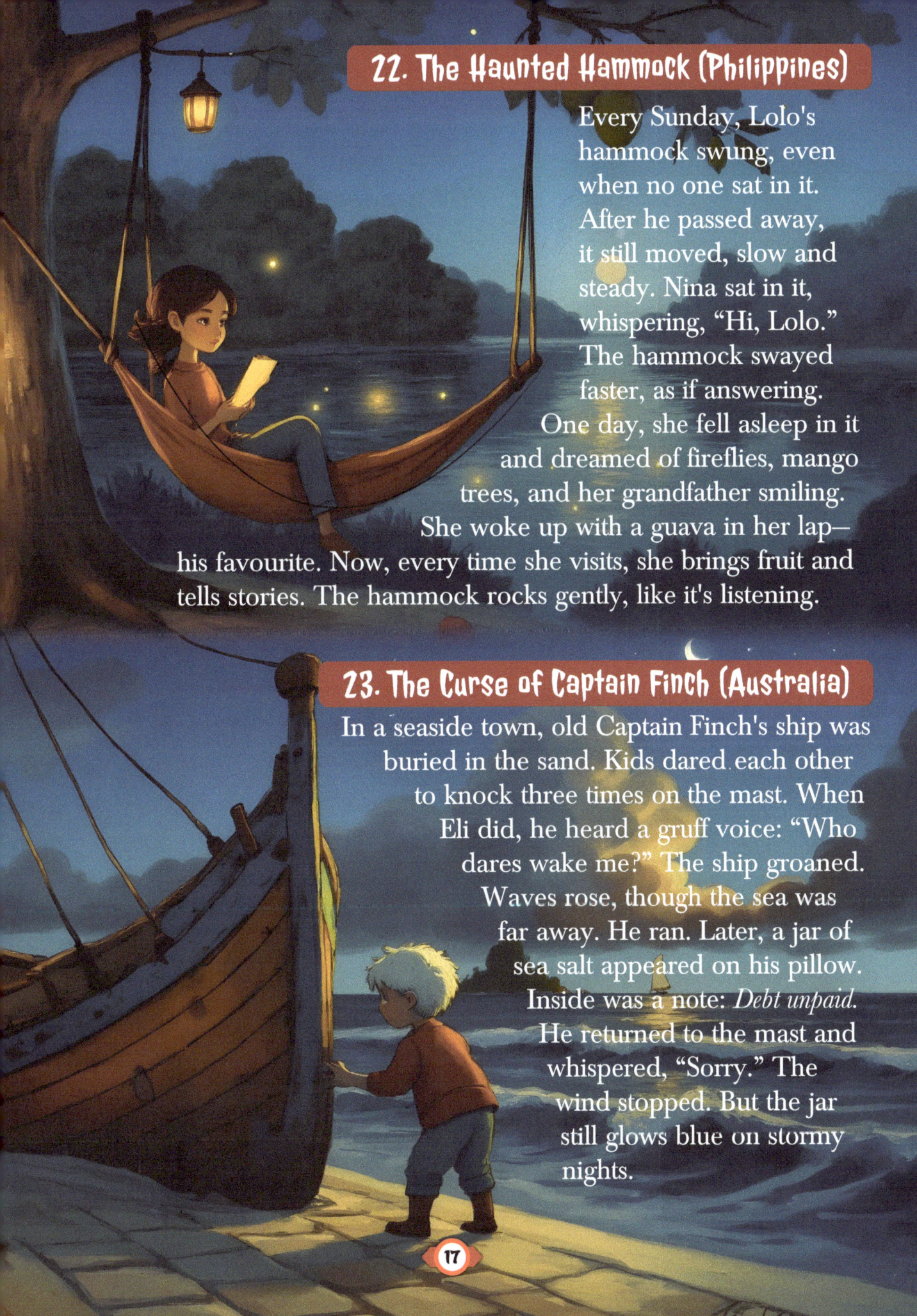

22. The Haunted Hammock (Philippines)

Every Sunday, Lolo's hammock swung, even when no one sat in it. After he passed away, it still moved, slow and steady. Nina sat in it, whispering, "Hi, Lolo." The hammock swayed faster, as if answering. One day, she fell asleep in it and dreamed of fireflies, mango trees, and her grandfather smiling. She woke up with a guava in her lap— his favourite. Now, every time she visits, she brings fruit and tells stories. The hammock rocks gently, like it's listening.

23. The Curse of Captain Finch (Australia)

In a seaside town, old Captain Finch's ship was buried in the sand. Kids dared each other to knock three times on the mast. When Eli did, he heard a gruff voice: "Who dares wake me?" The ship groaned. Waves rose, though the sea was far away. He ran. Later, a jar of sea salt appeared on his pillow. Inside was a note: *Debt unpaid.* He returned to the mast and whispered, "Sorry." The wind stopped. But the jar still glows blue on stormy nights.

24. The Starlight Ghost (Chile)

In the Atacama Desert, Ana saw a glowing girl every night staring at the stars. "I'm waiting for my family," she'd say. "They left on a starship." Ana thought she was pretending. But one evening, the ghost pointed up. A streak of light flashed across the sky. "They're back," she whispered—and vanished. Since then, Ana visits the same spot every year. Once, she found a silver charm in the sand shaped like a rocket. She wears it always, just in case someone's still watching the stars.

25. The Whispering Bed (Pakistan)

Tariq stayed at his cousin's home in Lahore. The bed creaked, even when empty. At midnight, it whispered, "Tell me a story." Startled, Tariq told a short tale. The bed sighed and was silent. Each night, it asked again. One night, he didn't respond—and heard crying. Soft, lonely. The next night, he told a bedtime story, and the bed rocked gently like a cradle. Before he left, the bed whispered, "Thank you." His cousin says it never made a sound again. Tariq still wonders who was listening.

26. The Tea House Visitor (China)

Li Mei served tea at her family's shop near the mountains. Every evening, a silent man in white robes entered, drank slowly, and left a coin. But the coin always vanished by morning. One day, she followed him. He walked into a fog and disappeared. In his place was a scroll with a poem: *Your tea warms hearts, even the forgotten ones.* Now, people say the tea shop feels extra cosy, like someone invisible is always watching, grateful for one last cup.

27. The Frozen School Bell (Iceland)

In Reykjavik, during winter, the school bell sometimes rings without reason. "Just wind," the teachers say. But when Freyja stayed late, she heard a voice: "Class time!" The hallway grew cold, and a shadowy teacher appeared, holding chalk. "Late again," she scolded. Freyja ran and never stayed after hours again. Every winter, the bell still rings on snowiest nights. And every year, a ghostly timetable appears on the blackboard—with names no one remembers.

28. The Puppet That Smiled (Turkey)

At a puppet shop in Istanbul, Yusuf saw a wooden puppet with sad eyes. He whispered, "I'll make you smile." That night, the puppet was in his bed, smiling. Frightened, Yusuf put it back. The next night, it danced. Each time he laughed, it smiled more. But one night, Yusuf cried— and the puppet's face twisted into sorrow. Now, it only reflects his emotions. He keeps it locked in a glass box, unsure who's copying whom.

29. The Bridge That Waits (USA)

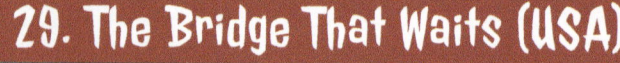

In Mississippi, there's a bridge locals call *The Waiter*. When Anaya crossed it one foggy evening, she heard footsteps behind her—exactly matching hers. She stopped. So did they. She ran. The bridge stretched longer. Finally, she shouted, "Please let me go!" A whisper replied, "You asked nicely." She landed on the far side in one step. Now, she warns others: Never run on that bridge. And always be polite.

30. The Clockwork Boy (Austria)

In Vienna, Eliza found a wind up boy in a locked museum case. She turned the key, and he blinked. "Name?" he asked. "Eliza," she said. "Friend," he replied. That night, he appeared in her dreams, building toy cities and laughing. But every morning, the toy was still behind glass. When she moved away, the boy whispered, "I'll wait." Years later, she visited again. The toy had vanished—but a small note sat in the case: *Eliza visited. I remember.*

31. The Fish in the Sky (Norway)

In a snowy village, Sindre saw glowing fish swimming through the night sky. No one else believed him. "Just stars," they said. One fish landed by his window, flapping gently. "We're lost," it whispered. Sindre pointed north. "That way." The fish winked and soared up. Next night, the sky shimmered with light. Northern Lights, people said. But Sindre saw the fish waving goodbye.

32. The Umbrella Girl (Japan)

Kaito left his umbrella at school. On the way home, rain poured—and a girl offered him her red one. "Take it," she said softly. Next morning, it was gone. Every rainy day after, she appeared with her umbrella, but never aged. He later found an old photo in the school's attic. There she was, standing in the rain—1954. "Lost in a storm," it read. Kaito still carries a red umbrella, in case she ever needs it back.

33. The Bread That Whistled (Italy)

In Rome, Nonna Rosa baked every morning. One day, the dough whistled before baking. "Don't joke," she told her grandson Nico. But when he listened, it hummed an old lullaby. That night, the bread cracked open with steam—and whispered, "Thanks for remembering." Nonna's face softened. "My mother used to sing that." The next day, the whistling stopped, but Nico swears one slice had a smiling face. They never threw away leftover bread again.

34. The Ghost at Table Seven (India)

In an old Delhi café, table seven was always clean but never sat at. "Reserved," said the waiter. One evening, Aarav dared to sit there. His tea turned ice-cold, and a chill brushed his neck. "You're not my usual guest," whispered a voice. Aarav leapt up. The waiter nodded. "She comes at 6. Every day. For 90 years." Now, a fresh rose waits there each evening. No one knows who brings it.

35. The Wailing Windmill (Netherlands)

Lena's village had a windmill that creaked only on windless nights. "It sings for lost dreams," her Oma said. One night, Lena heard a lullaby from its blades. Inside, dusty drawings of flying machines lined the walls. She added one of her own. The next morning, her drawing was gone—but the creaking had stopped. Since then, the windmill only sings when a dream is forgotten. Lena never forgets hers.

36. The Phantom Sandcastle (Maldives)

On the beach, Sami built a tall sandcastle. Next morning, it had towers he never made. Every day it grew: bridges, flags, windows. One evening, he saw a shadowy child shaping a turret. "It's almost ready," the ghost said. Then vanished. A wave washed it away that night. But the next morning, a message was written in the sand: *Thank you, King Sami.* He still builds castles, just in case the ghost wants to return.

37. The Chalkboard Scribbler (South Africa)

At a school in Cape Town, the chalkboard wrote by itself. "Learn from me," it scribbled in perfect cursive. Miss Themba thought it was a prank—until it solved complex sums nobody taught yet. Then poems. Then secrets. One day, it wrote: *Thank you for listening.* After that, it stopped. But the board still glows faintly at sunset. And sometimes... very softly... it hums.

38. The Lantern Parade (South Korea)

Every winter, Jiwoo saw floating lanterns drift through her village, long after the festival ended. One night, she followed them to a clearing—where glowing people danced silently. One lantern drifted into her hand. "Keep it safe," a whisper said. She lit it each year and never told anyone. Until her daughter saw the same parade. "They smiled at me," she said. Jiwoo only nodded. "They always do."

"Goodbye, Yannis."

39. The Goat Who Knew Names (Greece)

On a farm in Crete, Yannis had a goat who bleated names—
before anyone said them aloud. One day, it called "Pappou!"
before they heard of his granddad's return. Another day, it
cried, "Fire!" right before lightning struck the barn. Locals said
it was cursed. Others said blessed. One morning, the goat said,
"Goodbye, Yannis." It died peacefully that night. Yannis buried
it beneath an olive tree, where whispers still drift in the breeze.

40. The Ice Cream That Vanished (Mexico)

Lola bought a bright blue ice cream at a festival. It melted strangely—upwards, into the air. She followed the drips, which led to a mirror stall. In the glass, her reflection licked the cone and smiled. "Delicious," it said. Lola blinked—and it was gone. Her own cone now empty. Since then, she avoids mirror stalls. And blue ice cream.

41. The Suitcase Under the Stairs (Scotland)

Finlay found a dusty suitcase in his gran's attic. It rattled. When he opened it, fog poured out and formed a face. "Thank you," it whispered. Inside were old clothes, a compass, and a diary that wrote itself. Every page told ghostly adventures— set in places Finlay had never been. He reads it every night. It's still not finished.

42. The Shoe That Wandered (Vietnam)

Lien lost one shoe in the market. She cried, but her mum said it would turn up. That night, the shoe knocked at the door—muddy and slightly chewed. "Someone brought it back," her dad joked. Next morning, it was gone again. This happened for weeks. Always returned. Always dirtier. Then one night, it brought a feather, a pebble, and a leaf. "Thank you," whispered Lien. She never wore them again. But she kept the shoe by her window. Just in case it has more stories to tell.

43. The Girl in the Painting (Hungary)

In Budapest, Dani saw a painting of a girl in a red dress. Her eyes followed him around the gallery. That night, he dreamed she walked out of the frame and danced in his room. Every time he returned, her pose had changed—hand raised, dress twirling. When the painting disappeared one day, no one believed him. But his sketchpad now contains drawings he didn't make—each showing her smiling wider.

44. The Hiccups of Doom (Peru)

Mateo got hiccups during a school trip to Machu Picchu. "Hold your breath!" someone said. "Drink upside-down!" But every time he hiccuped, something weird happened—shadows flickered, birds stopped chirping. One hiccup cracked a rock. Terrified, he whispered, "Please stop." A low voice replied, "You called us." After that, the hiccups stopped. But he hears faint giggles in the wind now—like ancient spirits still laughing.

In a sleepy village, Nora noticed one puddle that didn't reflect the sky—it showed tomorrow. One day, it showed her dog escaping. The next day, it happened. Another time, it showed a rainbow before a storm. She told no one, afraid it would dry up. Then it showed her, older, holding a notebook. She smiled. The next day, she began writing stories. All inspired by puddles and little glimpses of what could be.

46. The Bed That Floated (Finland)

During the polar night, Aino's bed drifted upward. She wasn't dreaming. It floated gently through the ceiling, above snowy rooftops, guided by glowing owls. "You're kind," they whispered. "We're showing you our sky." Stars danced. Spirits glided. She returned to bed before dawn. No one believed her—until her room filled with snowy owl feathers. She keeps them in a box marked "Real."

In the attic, Sofia found a portrait of a little girl. Each month, the girl looked a bit older. One day, she winked. Another, she wore the same dress Sofia had just bought. "Are you... me?" she whispered. The next day, the girl was gone. The mirror nearby held her smile.

48. The Library Mouse (USA)

Every night, a tiny mouse scurried through the old town library. It squeaked at closed books—and they opened. Pages turned themselves. One night, Lily stayed late and saw it. "You like stories too?" she asked. The mouse nodded. She left cheese and a bookmark. Next day, the books she'd wanted were already on the desk. The librarian just smiled. "Our smallest helper works fast."

49. The Train that Never Stopped (Argentina)

Julián heard it every night—whistle, tracks, silence. But the nearest train station had been closed for decades. One foggy night, he saw lights flash past the fields. A shadowy train with empty windows. He waved. It slowed—but didn't stop. Just enough to toss a ticket onto the ground. *One ride. One wish.* He kept it in a shoebox. Still deciding.

50. The Pocket Watch That Tickled (Switzerland)

Luca found an old pocket watch that tickled when he held it. Not his hand—his heart. Every tick felt like a memory returning. He saw places he'd never been, faces he never met. "It remembers you," his grandfather said. "From before." Luca wore it always, even though it made him feel sad sometimes. Happy too. Like remembering a favourite dream you didn't know you had.

51. The Alley of Echoes (Singapore)

Mei took a shortcut home and heard footsteps copy hers—left, right, pause. But no one followed. "Who's there?" she asked. A whisper echoed, "Mei." She ran. The next day, she returned. "Do you want to walk with me?" The echo replied, "Yes." Now, every walk through the alley feels a little warmer. And safer. And never lonely.

52. The Mirror that Smiled First (Brazil)

Nina brushed her teeth and glanced at the mirror. Her reflection blinked—before she did. Then it smiled wider than possible. She gasped, and it froze. "Sorry," it mouthed. "Got excited." Now, every morning, her reflection grins early. It never copies her exactly. But it always looks like it's having fun. Nina waves back.

53. The Invisible Tea Party (England)

Lottie set up her dolls for tea. But when she returned with biscuits, five teacups were already full. "I didn't pour yet," she whispered. A napkin fluttered. Then a crumb disappeared mid-air. Every day after, one extra seat was filled—by no one she could see. But always someone who left polite little burps.

54. The Flying Coat (Russia)

Misha's winter coat kept going missing. He'd hang it up, but it'd flap away like it had wings. One night, he caught it sneaking out the window. "Going to help," it whispered. Next day, the paper said someone survived a storm—wrapped in a red coat. His coat. It came home muddy, but proud.

Going to help.

55. The Shadow with a Hat (Nigeria)

Zuri saw a shadow with a wide-brimmed hat follow her home. But when she turned, no one was there. That night, her dreams were filled with music and markets from long ago. "Ancestor," her gran whispered. "He's watching. That's good." Now, every time Zuri's scared, she looks behind her. The shadow's always there, just tipping its hat.

56. The Library That Rearranged Itself (Germany)

In Leipzig, a tiny library changed overnight. Books swapped shelves. Titles in languages no one spoke. Little Leo once whispered, "I wish I could read pirate stories." Next day, the whole front shelf was sea tales. One book even had sand inside. When Leo whispered thank you, the shelves swayed in a silent bow.

57. The Rattling Painting (Turkey)

Ay e's grandpa painted a boat that never moved—until one night, it rocked in the frame. Wind blew from the canvas. "Time to sail," whispered a voice. Ay e touched the painting and felt spray on her face. When she stepped back, her shoes were wet. Now, every full moon, the boat sails a little further.

"Time to sail"

58. The Sneezing Statue (France)

A marble lion in Paris sneezed one spring morning. Just once. Pollen, maybe. But ever since, tourists kept finding fresh paw prints around it. Chloe left a scarf on its paw for fun. Next morning, it was wrapped round its neck. She never saw it move. But it did wink in her dream.

59. The Bell That Rang Backwards (India)

At sunset, the temple bell tolled backwards—ding, then dong. Rohan counted thirteen rings, not twelve. "The spirit hour," the priest whispered. That night, Rohan saw a boy from the past, smiling in the smoke of incense. "Thanks for noticing," he said. Since then, Rohan always listens backwards. Some stories start at the end.

60. The Cat with Two Shadows (Morocco)

Youssef fed a scruffy cat behind his flat. One day, it had two shadows. One acted normal. The other danced. It bowed when Youssef blinked. "Ghost cat," his sister said. But it purred like any cat. Except sometimes, its second shadow stretched long, curling into letters: *Thank you for seeing me.*

61. The Whispering Fridge (USA)

Every time Dakota opened the fridge after midnight, it whispered. "More pickles," it once said. "Colder, please," another time. She tried unplugging it—but it hummed louder. She taped a note inside: *What do you want?* The next day, the ketchup bottle had a smiley face drawn in steam. She left it snacks after that.

62. The Blanket That Tucked Itself (Sweden)

Lina's blanket always ended up neatly tucked, even if she kicked it off. "Mum, did you fix it?" "No," her mum said. One night, Lina stayed half-awake. A glowing hand gently pulled the blanket up. "Good dreams," it whispered. She smiled. "Thanks." It still tucks her in—only if she's kind that day.

63. The Tunnel That Giggled (Mexico)

On the playground, there was a tiny tunnel slide that giggled when kids slid down. Only some heard it. "Ticklish," said little Clara. One day, she whispered a joke into it. The slide rumbled with laughter. The next day, stickers covered the slide—smiley faces, stars, ghosts. Clara giggled back.

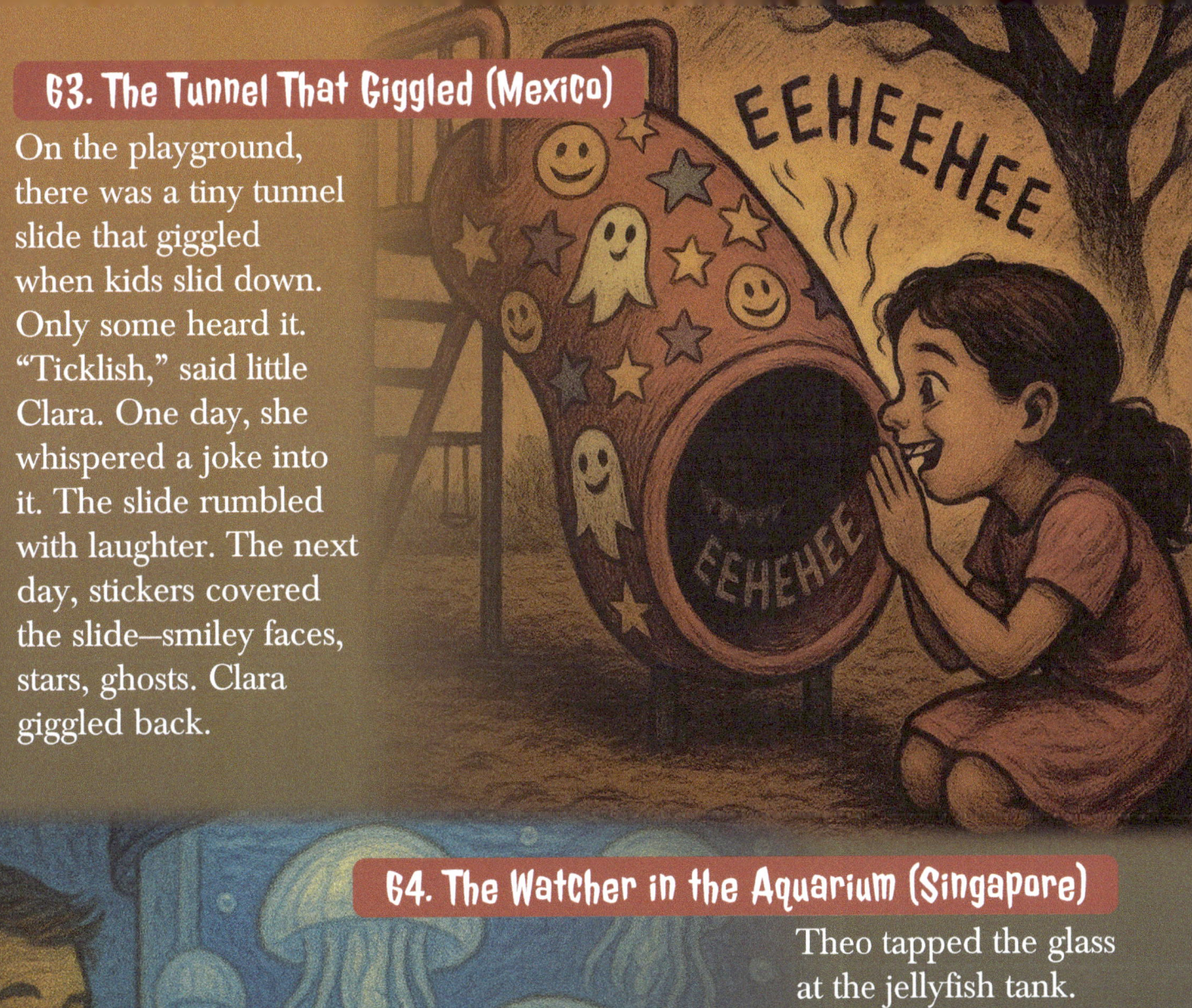

64. The Watcher in the Aquarium (Singapore)

Theo tapped the glass at the jellyfish tank. One jellyfish turned and blinked. Blinked. Then winked. "Dad, it looked at me!" "They don't have eyes," his dad said. But Theo waved anyway. Each time he returned, the same jellyfish swam up. Once, he left a drawing. It stayed stuck to the glass for weeks.

65. The Bus That Drove Through Dreams (Australia)

Ava dreamed of missing the school bus. Then the bus drove through her dream—real, glowing, full of kids sleeping. "Hop on," the driver said. Ava did. In the morning, she woke rested, shoes dusty. She found a bus pass in her hand. It read: *Route 9¾ – Sleep Express.*

66. The Clock That Counted Feelings (Ireland)

Liam's old clock ticked only when someone felt something strongly. It stayed silent for days, then ticked madly during a sad film. Once, it tocked when he was nervous for a test. Then stopped. "It doesn't keep time," his nan said. "It keeps *you*." Liam tickled it once. It giggled.

67. The Window that Reflected Stars (China)

In Mei's bedroom, her window never showed the street—just stars. Even in daylight. One night, she saw a shooting star zoom *inside* the room. "Make a wish," whispered the window. She wished for her grandma to visit her dreams. That night, they danced on the stars. The window still glows gently.

68. The Missing Sock Mystery (USA)

Max lost socks constantly. Always one of a pair. Then he found a note under his bed: *Borrowed for adventures. Will return washed.* Slowly, socks came back—faintly glowing, slightly softer. One had glitter. Another smelled like clouds. Max now leaves out spares, just in case they're needed.

BORROWED FOR ADVENTURES WILL RETURN WASHED

69. The Swing That Sang (South Korea)

In the park, one swing sang soft lullabies when the wind blew. No one else heard it. Jiho sat on it and whispered, "I like your songs." The swing swayed gently. "I like your smile," it replied. Now, whenever he's sad, he visits. The swing always sings—just for him.

70. The Fork That Pointed (Philippines)

At dinner, a silver fork spun on its own and pointed at plates. "Not that one," it warned once. The food was undercooked. It pointed again—towards Lola's cake. "Yes," it hummed. The family now treats the fork like royalty. It points. They follow. No one's ever gotten food poisoning again.

71. The Fog That Followed (Canada)

Ellie noticed fog following her after school. Just her. It curled around her bike. It wrapped her bag gently. "It likes you," said her granddad. "Old spirits love kind kids." One day, she sneezed and said, "Excuse me." The fog shaped into a heart. It still waits for her at the school gate.

72. The Tree That Hugged Back (New Zealand)

Mira hugged the giant pōhutukawa every morning. One windy day, it bent slightly—towards her. Leaves brushed her cheek like a kiss. From then on, when she hugged it, its bark felt warm. Once, she cried beneath it. Its branches rustled softly, dropping a blossom in her lap. "I love you too," she whispered.

73. The Music Box in the Lake (Switzerland)

Luca dropped a music box into Lake Geneva. It sank with a plop. He cried— until that night. The melody played softly outside his window. He peeked out. The lake glowed. The next day, the box was on his windowsill, damp but whole. Now it only plays at night. And only for him.

74. The Shoe That Danced Alone (Spain)

Carmen's flamenco shoe wouldn't sit still. At night, it tapped on the floor— click, clack, spin. One morning, it wore a tiny red ribbon that no one put there. "Was that... a ghost duet?" her cousin asked. Carmen nodded. The other shoe finally joined in. Now they both dance at midnight.

75. The Umbrella That Followed Rain (Japan)

Hana lost her red umbrella. Days later, she saw it bobbing behind a stranger—no hand holding it. She followed it through the drizzle. It paused at her door and tipped a little, like a bow. Since then, whenever Hana forgets her umbrella, it shows up—hovering, faithful, always dry inside.

76. The Lemonade Stand That Served Spirits (USA)

Toby set up a lemonade stand. But customers kept appearing... fuzzy. Pale. Floating. "One cup, please," they'd whisper. They paid in buttons and mist. Toby didn't mind—his till always felt full. One ghost saluted him: "Best lemonade in the afterlife." The sign now reads: *Open to All (Living or Not).*

77. The Backpack with Secrets (South Africa)

Nia's backpack zipped and unzipped on its own. One day, she found a pebble inside—shaped like a heart. Another time, a note: *You're brave.* She started talking to it. "Thanks." The backpack rustled in reply. Her friend swears it growled at a bully once. "That's my bag," Nia said. "It's got my back."

78. The Hallway That Shifted (Egypt)

Kareem's school had a hallway that led somewhere new each week. One day, it ended in sand dunes. Another time, stars. Only Kareem ever noticed. "You again?" the hallway whispered once. He grinned. "Take me somewhere cool." It led him to a room of ancient scrolls. "Just don't tell the headteacher."

79. The Fish That Spoke Dreams (Thailand)

Lulu caught a shimmering fish and heard a tiny voice: *Set me free, and I'll share your dreams.* She did. That night, she dreamt of flying elephants and floating gardens. Every night after, the fish swam by her window, whispering, "Tonight's dream is a surprise." She always woke smiling.

Set me free, and I'll share your dreams

80. The Quilt That Changed Stories (Wales)

Gran's patchwork quilt showed different pictures each night. A dragon one night, a ghost dog the next. Emrys traced the shapes with his finger. "Are you telling me bedtime stories?" he whispered. The quilt warmed. "Thank you." From then on, the stories stitched themselves before his eyes.

81. The Notebook That Wrote Itself (Pakistan)

Zara found an old notebook in the attic. Blank—until she opened it again. Words flowed across the page in swirling ink: *You found me. Want to write together?* She nodded. Now, every day, they write poems and ghost stories. She never told anyone. But the notebook always signs them: $Z + Z$

82. The Cookie Jar With a Bite (Italy)

Marco reached for a cookie and yelped— it bit him! Just a tiny nibble. "Don't be rude," his Nonna said. "Say please." He tried again, this time with manners. The jar opened itself. Since then, it only bites when someone's greedy. Marco warns his friends: *Be nice, or it'll nibble you too.*

83. The Ladder to the Sky (Scotland)

Eilidh found a rope ladder in the woods, tied to nothing—just hanging in mid-air. She climbed. Clouds tickled her face. At the top: a floating island with sheep made of mist. She had tea with them. When she came down, her shoes were wet with dew. "Don't tell," whispered the wind.

"It's broken," he frowned.

84. The Balloon That Didn't Float (Greece)

Niko's balloon floated downward. "It's broken," he frowned. But it tugged gently toward the hills. He followed. It led him to a hidden grove full of tiny glowing lights. "Thanks," he whispered. The balloon finally rose— high and proud. Now, every year, he lets one go, hoping to lead someone else.

85. The Boat in the Bathtub (Vietnam)

Linh's toy boat drifted to the drain—and vanished. That night, she dreamed of sailing through underground rivers, with glowing fish and paper lanterns. The boat returned the next day, wet but glowing. She set it afloat again. Now her dreams are always full of water and wonders.

86. The Shoes That Led the Way (Kenya)

Milo's muddy shoes moved by themselves, pointing towards forgotten paths. He followed once and found a tiny kitten stuck in a bush. Another time, a dropped wallet. He kept the shoes clean and thanked them daily. When he outgrew them, he whispered, "Find someone new." They vanished the next morning.

87. The Fireplace That Giggled (Ireland)

Maeve's fireplace giggled during storms. Not crackled—*giggled*. One night, she tossed in a marshmallow. The flames squealed with delight. From then on, she fed it little snacks. Raisins, biscuits, tiny letters. The fire always responded with laughter and warmth. "It likes you," said her brother. "Of course," Maeve said. "I'm kindling."

88. The Headphones That Played Memories (South Korea)

Jin found a pair of headphones on a park bench. When he put them on, he heard laughter—his mum's, from when he was five. Then his granddad's stories. The next day, the voices were from someone else's memories. Jin left them on the bench again. Sharing magic is polite.

89. The Broom That Cleaned Secrets (Hungary)

Eva's broom swept even when she wasn't holding it. Once, it revealed a message in the dust: *I know what you did—nice job hiding the cake.* She laughed. The broom only cleaned where secrets were buried. Now, Eva always checks after sweeping. "Got anything juicy today?" she asks. Sometimes... it nods.

I KNOW WHAT YOU DID—NICE JOB HIDING THE CAKE

90. The Bell That Called the Kind (India)

A tiny bell outside the temple rang on its own— only when someone kind walked past. It never rang for bullies. One day, it rang three times for little Ravi. "You've got a strong heart," said the old priest. Ravi beamed. Now he visits daily. The bell always sings for him.

91. The Whispering Comb (Egypt)

In Cairo, Amira found a golden comb in a street market. That night, her hair brushed itself, gently, as a voice whispered lullabies in ancient words. She dreamed of deserts and queens. Her grandma gasped when she saw it. "That belonged to someone royal," she said. The next night, Amira placed the comb on her pillow and whispered, "Thank you." The whispers stopped—but every time she combs her hair, it shines like desert sun.

92. The Puppet That Blinked (Czech Republic)

At the Prague puppet shop, Theo spotted one puppet—tall hat, crooked smile—that blinked at him. "That one's not for sale," the old man muttered. But when Theo returned, the puppet was gone. That night, something tapped at his window. There it was—dangling from invisible strings, grinning. "I chose you," it whispered. Theo let it in. Every night, they practised secret puppet shows. The puppet danced on its own, told stories in strange voices, and once sewed its own tiny shoes. When Theo tried to tell someone, the puppet froze like wood again. "Shhh," it said. "Magic hates attention."

93. The Feather That Followed (New Zealand)

In a Māori village, Anika found a glowing feather. She tucked it in her pocket. That night, she dreamt of flying through ancient forests, guided by a giant bird with eyes like stars. In the morning, the feather hovered above her pillow. It never stayed still—fluttering ahead of her steps, hiding in her socks, or landing in her lunchbox. She once lost it, and the wind howled for hours. When she found it again, it spun wildly, then calmed. Her gran smiled. "It's chosen you. It'll leave when you're brave enough to fly." Anika held it tighter. "Not just yet."

Niamh always counted eleven stairs to her bedroom. But some nights, there were twelve. The twelfth creaked differently—cold underfoot. One night, she looked back. The staircase stretched down into blackness, far deeper than the house allowed. From below, soft footsteps echoed up. "You forgot me," a voice whispered. Niamh ran to bed. The next morning, only eleven steps again. She placed a toy on the twelfth step one evening. It vanished. That night, her toy returned—with new buttons sewn on. "Play again?" said the step. Niamh smiled, nervously. "Maybe tomorrow." The step creaked—almost like laughter—as it vanished again.

95. The Doll's Tea Party (India)

Priya set out plastic cups for her dolls. "Tea time!" she chirped. But when she turned around, the cups were full of chai—steaming. Her dolls had shifted slightly, arms out, heads tilted. She blinked. "Mum?" "I didn't touch anything," her mum said. That night, tiny clinks echoed from her toy shelf. The next morning, crumbs dotted the dollhouse table, and one doll had a sugar cube on its lap. Curious, Priya left a biscuit. It vanished. The dolls looked... grateful. Once, she peeked through the keyhole at midnight. They were sipping. One turned, smiled, and raised a teacup to her.

96. The Empty Chair at Campfire Hill (Canada)

Every summer, campers told scary stories at Campfire Hill. There was always one extra chair. "It's for the Listener," the counsellor joked. "He's harmless." Kids laughed—until the chair creaked on its own. One year, Mia stayed behind to collect marshmallows. Alone, she saw a shadowy boy warming his hands by the fire. "Good stories tonight," he said. Then vanished. She found a marshmallow beside the empty chair, perfectly roasted. From then on, she brought extras—one for the Listener. He never missed a night. Sometimes, the flames flickered blue when he liked the tale. Mia always told the spookiest ones.

97. The Crayons That Drew Without Her (South Korea)

Min-Jun loved to draw. One day, she left her crayons on the floor. When she returned, a dragon filled the page—one she hadn't drawn. Every morning, new sketches appeared: ghost cats, flying dumplings, a haunted piano. She tried hiding the crayons, but they rattled in the drawer until released. One night, she stayed awake, pretending to sleep. At midnight, the crayons stood upright, glowing. They whispered, sketched, giggled. "We missed her," said blue. Min-Jun sat up. "You draw dreams, don't you?" They froze. Then yellow said, "We like yours best." Since then, she always leaves them paper—and a thank you.

98. The Clock That Skipped Time (Germany)

Felix's cuckoo clock chirped thirteen times—once more than it should. That day, time felt strange. His walk to school took seconds. Lunch break lasted hours. When he asked his grandpa, he just said, "The clock gives time to those who need it." Felix tested it—wishing for longer dreams, shorter tests. It worked. But one day, he asked for too much, and everything froze. Birds paused mid-air. Rain hung like glass. "Time's not a toy," whispered the cuckoo bird. "Be kind with your seconds." Felix nodded. From then on, he only used the extra tick to say thank you—and hug his grandpa.

99. The Dream That Leaked Into Daylight (Brazil)

Rafa dreamt of a carnival—ghost floats, glittering shadows, music made of whispers. When he woke, glitter covered his sheets. Confused, he checked his window: feathers on the sill, a mask beneath his pillow. The next night, he joined the dance again, spinning with translucent dancers and floating lanterns. Each morning, more dream-things appeared: confetti, candles, candy no one sold. His mum noticed. "You've been somewhere special." He nodded. On the final night of carnival, a dream-float bowed to him. "Thank you for believing." The next morning, the bedroom was normal again. Except the music still hummed softly in the mirror.

100. The Ghost Who Lost Her Name (Japan)

In the village shrine, Aiko heard a voice: "Have you seen my name?" She turned—no one there. Each day, the voice followed. Gentle. Lonely. "Help me remember." Aiko left paper slips with names: Hana, Sora, Yuki. The spirit would hum happily, then fall silent. Until one day: "Yes. That's me." The wind shifted. Cherry blossoms bloomed, out of season. "Thank you," the voice whispered. From then on, the shrine bell rang once every morning—though no one pulled the rope. Aiko smiled. She never told anyone the name. It was a secret between her and the girl who remembered herself.

101. The Final Page (Nowhere and Everywhere)

You turn the last page of this book. A soft breeze stirs, though the windows are closed. Somewhere, a whisper: "You've read about us. Now we know you too." Your lights flicker. Just once. Maybe. In your room, something shifts slightly. A shadow that wasn't there a moment ago. Don't worry—it's a friendly ghost. One who loves stories, like you. It might nudge a bookmark, or leave a toy sideways. Tonight, if you hear a giggle or creak, just smile. Close your eyes. Whisper: "Thanks for reading with me." You'll hear it back: *"Thanks for letting us in."*